NICK JR.
DORA the EXPLORER®

Dora Climbs Star Mountain

adapted by Alison Inches
illustrated by A&J Studios

SIMON AND SCHUSTER/NICKELODEON

Based on the TV series *Dora the Explorer* as seen on Nick Jr.

SIMON AND SCHUSTER
First published in Great Britain in 2007 by Simon & Schuster UK Ltd
1st Floor, 222 Gray's Inn Road, London WC1X 8HB
A CBS COMPANY

Originally published in the USA in 2007 by Simon Spotlight,
an imprint of Simon & Schuster Children's Division, New York.

A CIP catalogue record for this book is available from the British Library

ISBN 978-0-85707-421-8

Printed in China

10 9 8 7 6 5 4 3

Visit our websites: www.simonandschuster.co.uk
www.nickjr.co.uk

iHola! I'm Dora, and this is my best friend, Boots. Today I got a present from my grandma. *Mi abuela* made me a necklace to match my bracelet. I really love it! Do you like presents too?

Uh-oh, that sounds like Swiper the Fox! That sneaky fox will try to swipe my necklace. If you see Swiper, say "Swiper, no . . ."

Oh, no! We're too late. Swiper swiped my necklace and threw it to the top of Star Mountain. I really love my necklace. Will you help Boots and me to get it back? Great!

Star Mountain is where the Explorer Stars live. If we call them, they will help us find my necklace. To call the Explorer Stars, we have to say *"Estrellas."* Say it with us. *"¡Estrellas!"*

Look! The Explorer Stars came! There's Tool Star, the Explorer Star with lots of tools. And there is Saltador, the super jumping Explorer Star. And there is Glowy, the bright light Explorer Star. The Explorer Stars will help us get my necklace back.

First we have to work out how to get to the top of Star Mountain. Who do we ask for help when we don't know which way to go? Map! Say "Map!"

Map says that to get my necklace back, we have to run up fifteen steps. Then we have to climb all the way up the Diamond. And that's how we'll get to the Giant Star on top of Star Mountain.

Can you see the steps? *¿Dónde están?* There they are! But they're covered in fog! We need Tool Star to help us through the fog. Which tool can Tool Star use to get us through the fog? *¡Sí!* A fan!

Tool Star is fanning the fog out of the way. Good fanning!

We made it through the fog to the steps. Count the fifteen steps with me. *Uno, dos, tres, cuatro, cinco, seis, siete, ocho, nueve, diez, once, doce, trece, catorce, quince.*

Great counting! We made it up all fifteen steps. But look at all this bubbling green goo! It's blocking our way! We need an Explorer Star to help us get past this goo. Glowy, the bright light Star, can help us melt the goo with her hot lights. Go, Glowy!

Yay! We made it past the goo! So where do we go next? Yeah, the Diamond! Wait, I hear a rumbling sound. It's a giant rock!

Look! It's Saltador, the super jumping Explorer Star. Saltador can help us jump over the falling rock. Let's jump on the count of three. Count with me. *¡Uno, dos, TRES!* We jumped over the giant rock! *¡Gracias, Saltador!*

Now let's use these star handles to climb the Diamond. The stars are red and green, *roja y verde.* We have to follow the pattern to climb to the top. Will you help? Say *"¡Roja! ¡Verde! ¡Roja! ¡Verde!"* Good job!

We made it up the Diamond! Thanks for helping. Now we need to go to the Giant Star to get my necklace back. *¿Dónde está?*

There's the Giant Star! And there's my necklace! To get up the Giant Star, we're going to need a long rope. Will you check Backpack for a long rope? You have to say "Backpack!"

Can you see a long rope? *¡Muy bien!* Very good! Thanks!

Now I have to throw the rope to the top of the Giant Star.
Wish me luck! Say *"¡Buena suerte!"*
Wow, I did it! Thanks for your help!

Now I have to grab the rope and climb to the top. Will you help me climb? Say *"¡Sube! ¡Sube, sube, sube!"* Great climbing! Can you see my necklace?

I see it! My necklace! My necklace!

¡Lo hicimos! We did it! You helped me get back my necklace, and the Explorer Stars helped too. *¡Gracias, estrellas!*

I couldn't have done it without you. *¡Gracias!* Thanks for helping!